WELCOME TO
PASSPORT TO READING
A beginning reader's ticket to a brand-new world!

Every book in this program is designed to build read-along and read-alone skills, level by level, through engaging and enriching stories. As the reader turns each page, he or she will become more confident with new vocabulary, sight words, and comprehension.

These PASSPORT TO READING levels will help you choose the perfect book for every reader.

READING TOGETHER
Read short words in simple sentence structures together to begin a reader's journey.

READING OUT LOUD
Encourage developing readers to sound out words in more complex stories with simple vocabulary.

READING INDEPENDENTLY
Newly independent readers gain confidence reading more complex sentences with higher word counts.

READY TO READ MORE
Readers prepare for chapter books with fewer illustrations and longer paragraphs.

This book features sight words from the educator-supported Dolch Sight Words List. This encourages the reader to recognize commonly used vocabulary words, increasing reading speed and fluency.

For more information, please visit lbyr.com/passporttoreading.

Enjoy the journey!

Cover design by Elaine Lopez-Levine. Cover illustration by Artful Doodlers.

Little, Brown and Company
Hachette Book Group
1290 Avenue of the Americas, New York, NY 10104
Visit us at LBYR.com

First Edition: July 2020

Little, Brown and Company is a division of Hachette Book Group, Inc.
The Little, Brown name and logo are trademarks of Hachette Book Group, Inc.

The publisher is not responsible for websites (or their content)
that are not owned by the publisher.

Library of Congress Control Number 2019947893

ISBNs: 978-0-316-49591-2 (pbk.), 978-0-316-49594-3 (ebook),
978-0-316-49595-0 (ebook), 978-0-316-49592-9 (ebook)

Printed in China

APS

10 9 8 7 6 5 4 3 2 1

Passport to Reading titles are leveled by independent reviewers applying the standards developed by Irene Fountas and Gay Su Pinnell in *Matching Books to Readers: Using Leveled Books in Guided Reading*, Heinemann, 1999.

OFFICIAL
MARK OF
SPIRIT

A Tricky Halloween

Adapted by Ellie Rose

L B

LITTLE, BROWN AND COMPANY
New York   Boston

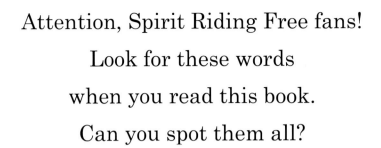

Attention, Spirit Riding Free fans!
Look for these words
when you read this book.
Can you spot them all?

initials

invitation

balloon

ghost

Halloween is very
spooky in Miradero.

Lucky wears a scary mask.

"Boo!" she shouts.

She scares Aunt Cora!

Lucky thinks being scared
on Halloween is fun.

"It is not fun!"
says Abigail.
"Snips scares
me too much!"

Lucky, Pru, and Abigail
want to play a trick on Snips.
It will teach him a lesson.

The PALs have an idea.
The legend of Sadie Crouthers
will help them trick Snips.

Sadie's birthday was on Halloween.
She never had a birthday party.

Her friends were always
too busy trick-or-treating.

Now Sadie's ghost looks
for kids to come to her
birthday party every year!

11

The PALs tell Snips about Sadie Crouthers.

They even show
him Sadie's necklace.
"What are those
letters?" Snips asks.

"Those are initials," says Lucky.
"They stand for a name,
like Sadie Crouthers."

"Or Señor Carrots!" Snips shouts.
Señor Carrots is his donkey.

Snips wants to give the
necklace to Señor Carrots.

"Sadie's ghost will haunt
you if you take the
necklace," Pru warns.

Later, Snips takes
the necklace anyway!

He goes to the barn to
give it to Señor Carrots.

The donkey is missing!
There is an invitation
to Sadie's birthday
party in his place.

Snips has to find his donkey!
He runs past Bianca
and Mary Pat.

"A ghost named Sadie
took Señor Carrots," says Snips.
"I am going to her birthday
party to save him!"

"We will give you a ride!" says Bianca.

Meanwhile, Pru and Abigail leave
a trail of carrots and hoof prints.

Snips, Bianca,
and Mary Pat
follow the trail.

It leads them past a creepy
balloon and a bunch of bats.

None of the PALs'
pranks scare Snips!

Soon, Snips and
the twins see
a spooky light.

It leads them to a cake.

It must be Sadie Crouthers's birthday cake!

"Welcome to my birthday party,"
says a spooky voice.
It is Lucky speaking into a bucket.
Her voice sounds extra creepy!

Now Snips is
really scared!

He puts Sadie's stolen
necklace on the table.

"Take it back!
Just give me Señor Carrots!"
says Snips.

"Promise you will not
scare your sister anymore!"
Lucky says in her ghost voice.

"I promise!"
Snips shouts.
There is a big cloud
of purple smoke.

Señor Carrots appears!
Snips is so happy.

The PALs' plan works!
Snips is scared!

But Lucky wants
to be scared, too.

Just then, the PALs see a ghost horse!
It is pulling a girl in a wagon.

Is it a real ghost?

The girls are scared.
They run away.

"Trick-or-treat!"
someone shouts.

It is Turo and Maricela!

They pranked the PALs!

"Happy Halloween!"
Turo and Maricela say.

It is the best Halloween ever!